Pet Peeves

by Sarah Willson
illustrated by John Nez

Kane Press, Inc.
New York

Library of Congress Cataloging-in-Publication Data

Willson, Sarah.
  Pet peeves / by Sarah Willson ; illustrated by John Nez.
    p. cm. — (Social studies connects)
  "Economics - grades: 1–3."
  Summary: A nine-year-old starts a pet-sitting business with his bossy big brother and ends up going on strike.
  ISBN 1-57565-149-1 (pbk. : alk. paper)
  [1. Brothers—Fiction. 2. Moneymaking projects—Fiction. 3. Pet sitting—Fiction.] I. Nez, John A., ill. II. Title. III. Series.
  PZ7.W6845Pe 2005
  [E]—dc22
                                    2004016962

10 9 8 7 6 5 4 3 2 1

First published in the United States of America in 2005 by Kane Press, Inc.
Printed in Hong Kong.

Social Studies Connects is a trademark of Kane Press, Inc.

Book Design: Edward Miller

www.kanepress.com

"See you kids later!" said Brad. He was zipping up his new jacket as he hurried off.

My friend Sue looked puzzled. "How come your brother has money to buy new stuff and you don't?"

I sighed. "Brad's old enough to have a job."

"Must be nice to have money," Sue said. "I wanted to go to soccer camp this summer, but the price went up, so we can't afford it."

"Yeah, I could sure use a new glove," I said. "This one's a wreck. No wonder I drop every fly ball."

"Hey!" Sue said. "Maybe we can find a way to pay for my camp and your glove ourselves!"

"We're too young to have real jobs," I pointed out. "And we can't rob a bank, since neither of us can drive a getaway car."

"Dennis, be serious," said Sue. "Let's try to think of a job we really could do."

We took a walk and talked it over. "We could help Brad with his paper route," suggested Sue.

"He'd never go for it," I scoffed. "There'd be less money for him. Have you noticed how he's been buying new clothes and stuff? I think he's got a crush on some girl named Lisa."

Sue giggled.

"How about babysitting?" she said.

"We're only nine," I reminded her.

Mr. Braga hurried by with his dog, Sparky. "I wish I had a dog," I said for the hundredth time.

"You'd get tired of walking him," Sue said.

"No way. Not if . . ." I stopped. "That's it!" I yelled. "Let's start a pet-care business!"

"It just might work," Sue said.

"Of course it will! And it might show my mom that I can take care of a dog of my own."

I can't play now, Sparky. I have to get to work.

Free enterprise means you have the freedom to start and run a business. Anybody can start a business. First you need a good idea. Dennis likes dogs— so he thinks of pet sitting. What are your interests?

We were busy making plans when Brad came back. He had a goofy new haircut. Sue and I looked at each other and grinned.

"What are you guys up to?" he asked.

"We're starting a pet-care business," I said.

"Cool!" said Brad. "How are you going to do it?"

"By making signs," I answered. "We'll just put them up and wait for people to call."

Every business sells something. Some businesses sell **goods**—things like books and toys. A supermarket sells groceries. A shoe store sells shoes!

"Call where?" asked Brad. "Mom will never let you use our home number."

Brad was right. He'd gotten his own phone with his paper-route money. Mom had told him he tied up the home phone too much.

"My mom will say the same thing about our phone," Sue said.

"Could we use yours?" I asked Brad.

"Of course," he said.

Some businesses sell **services**—things people do for other people. Babysitters are paid to take care of kids. Dentists are paid to fix teeth!

9

I was suspicious. Brad had agreed too quickly.

"And," he went on, "I'd even be willing to answer the phone for you. All you have to do is pay me half the money the business makes."

"*Half*?" I gasped.

"That's the deal. Phone lines cost a lot."

What could we do? We had to have a phone. So we said okay.

We picked a name for our business and made a cool sign. It was hard to figure out what to charge. So we looked up pet sitters in the phone book and called a few. Since we were just starting out, we made our prices low.

LET US HELP CARE FOR YOUR PET!

NO JOB TOO SMALL OR TOO STINKY!

WE LOVE ALL ANIMALS! EVEN REPTILES!

Please call 555-5562

Dog walking: $2 per walk
Cat care: $3/day
(includes feeding and litter-box changing)

Turtles, gerbils, rabbits, birds and other pets: please call for rates

Advertising is all the different ways you let people know about your business. Businesses advertise in lots of ways—with flyers and billboards, on the radio and TV, in newspapers and magazines.

We used Brad's printer to make a whole bunch of copies. He only charged us for the paper.

Sue and I put the ads in the vet's office, in the park, in the pet shop, and in the supermarket.

Marketing is how you plan to sell something. You think about who will want to buy what you are selling and how to get their attention. For example, you can set up a lemonade stand where thirsty people walk by—like near a park on a hot day.

The ads worked!

Brad's phone started ringing. Lots of people needed dog walkers, cat sitters, and gerbil feeders. Someone even asked us to take care of his pet boa constrictor!

Sue and I got up early every day to walk dogs and feed cats. Brad slept late. He said his job was answering the phone when customers called. He was probably hoping someone else might call, too—someone named Lisa.

Hello, this is Purrfect Pet-Sitters!

A **customer** is someone who buys your goods or services. If you want your business to make money, you need customers!

"I think it's wonderful that the kids are working together so nicely!" I heard my mother say.

"Yes, and how sweet of Brad to lend a hand," I heard Sue's mother answer.

We put up more ads and made special T-shirts. Soon we had more business than we could handle. Since I like dogs, Sue let me take the dog jobs.

"How was dog walking?" she asked me.

"Fine," I said, "except I had to walk four dogs at a time and they all decided to chase a squirrel in the pouring rain."

If you have a business, you have costs—like advertising. The money you make after you subtract your costs is called your **profit**.

"How was the Hermans' snake?" I asked.

"Okay, but he escaped and it took me forever to find him. And then I had to hurry up and feed the Mayers' parrot, play with the Wongs' ferrets, and clean the Adams's slimy fish tank. I'm tired."

Just then we heard Brad yell, "Sue! Dennis!" He handed each of us two more messages.

"I can't be two places at once!" wailed Sue.

"Why can't *you* do a few jobs?" I asked Brad.

"Someone has to answer the phone," Brad said.

"Let's take turns," Sue said.

Brad just shrugged. "That's not our deal." He began sorting the money into piles—a big one for himself and two small ones for Sue and me.

"Maybe we could hire my kid sister, Claire, and her friends," said Sue. "They could do the easy stuff, like filling water bowls."

"Great idea!" I said.

"Okay," said Brad. "But their pay has to come out of your part of the money!"

Sue and I just looked at each other.

The little kids were thrilled to be Junior Pet-Sitters. Having them help out did make things easier—but not for long.

The business kept growing! And Brad kept turning us down when we asked him to do some of the pet sitting.

A business gets bigger when it gets more customers or when customers buy more. One happy customer leads to another. When customers are pleased, they tell their friends.

"Soccer camp starts in two weeks!" said Sue a
few days later. "And I haven't even made *half* the
money I need."

I nodded gloomily. "I'm not even close to being
able to buy a new glove. Brad's just not being fair."

"It's time to do something," said Sue.

We called the little kids together for a meeting.
"We think it's time to go on strike," Sue said.
"What's a strike?" asked Claire.
"It's when a group of workers gets together and agrees to stop working," Sue explained.

A **strike** is when workers walk off their jobs. It's a way of trying to get what they want—such as higher pay or more time off. Sometimes strikers win—and sometimes they don't!

"We want Brad to do his fair share of the work, and give us our fair share of the money," I said. "He keeps saying no, so we'll all stop pet sitting until he listens."

"Hooray!" cheered the younger kids. I don't think they really understood, but I guess a strike sounded like fun.

Nobody really *wants* to go on strike. But workers do it when talks with their bosses fail.

The next morning, we began to picket.

Brad poked his head out the window. "What's all the noise? My phone's been ringing non-stop and I can't hear . . ." His voice trailed off as he read our signs.

Want Clean Kitty Litter? Pay the Kitty Sitter!

We dog walkers are ready to walk!

Strike

A **picket line** is a line of people on strike.
Sometimes the picketers carry signs.
They make up chants like:
1-2-3-4, we won't take this anymore!
5-6-7-8, pay us more, we won't wait!

"We're on strike!" said Claire cheerfully.
"We're protesting unfair labor practices," I said.
Brad looked at me. "You and Sue come inside.
Let's talk this over before our customers see
these signs."

We had a long talk. We told Brad we couldn't handle all the work by ourselves. This time he really listened. Then we made a new deal. And oh, yeah—we gave the little kids a raise.

PURRFECT PET-SITTERS'
NEW RULES

1. Brad, Dennis and Sue will take turns answering the phone and doing pet jobs.
2. Brad, Dennis and Sue will each get an equal share of the profits.
3. Brad, Dennis and Sue will share all the costs.
4. Brad, Dennis and Sue will chip in and pay the little kids.

We all went outside. "Strike's over! We won!" I yelled. Everybody cheered.

"Why do you think Brad gave in so fast?" Sue asked me.

"He quit his paper route last week, so now being a Purrfect Pet-Sitter is the only way he has to earn money. Besides, Brad knew he was wrong."

Talking about something to try to reach an agreement is called **negotiating**. When people negotiate, they try to make a decision that is fair to everyone.

A few weeks later, Sue and I were on my front stoop. She'd spent the morning at soccer camp. I'd been playing ball—with my new glove. We had more free time now that Brad was pet sitting, too.

"Brad has been so nice to us lately!" said Sue.

"Yeah," I agreed. "Maybe it's because Lisa started calling him back."

"Shhh! Here he comes now," Sue whispered.

"Hi, guys," said Brad.
"Hi," I replied. "What's in the box?"
"Oh, this?" he said. "It's a present for you."
Did I hear right? For me? I opened it up.

"A *puppy*!" I shouted.

"It's a bonus for all your hard work," Brad said. "And Lisa and I will even walk him for you—absolutely free!"

MAKING CONNECTIONS

Being a Purrfect Pet-Sitter is no walk in the park—until everyone learns to work together! Dennis and Sue have to brainstorm ways to earn money. Then, they have to cooperate with Brad to turn their idea into a real business.

Look Back
- Look at pages 4–7. Describe how Dennis and Sue come up with the idea for Purrfect Pet-Sitters.
- On pages 9 and 10, how does Brad get involved? What will his job be?
- Look at pages 16 and 17. How do Dennis and Sue divide up the work?
- Read page 26. Look at the Purrfect Pet-Sitters' New Rules. How does everyone's job change? Do you think this plan will work better? Why?

Try This!
Pretend You're Starting a Business!

Work together with a friend. Brainstorm ideas. Decide what you'd like to do. For example, you could start a lemonade and snack stand. You could wash cars or do yard work. You might even design your own greeting cards on the computer!

Once you've decided on a business, make a plan. How much would you charge? How would you divide the work? The pay? The expenses? How would you schedule your time? When problems come up, how would you solve them?